The Adventures Of Crazy Daisy And Disaster Casper

Getting Our Guard

Kristen Stafford

Preface

There sometimes comes a moment when you think you have a great idea, and then later find yourself saying "What was I thinking!?". When I became a single mother I was living in another state 7 hours away from my family and friends. I felt a lot of overwhelming feelings, but my only concern was being the best mom I could through all of life's obstacles. As if I didn't have enough on my plate already, I decided it would be good for my daughter, Daisy, if we got a dog. Life has been a riot since, and the adventures forever have pressed their memories in my heart- whether it be getting stuck on top of a mountain or simply trying to get ready for bed. When I didn't have anyone to share the stories with, I decided I would share them with the world. This one is just the beginning. I hope all of you out there who can relate find humor, joy, and strength in both my stories and the adventures that unfold in your life.

Yes, the stories are real.

Dedicated to our dog, Casper,
who gave us peace, security, rest, fun
and love when we needed it the most.

When I was just 4,
I lived in a house surrounded by trees.
An old noisy place just my momma and me.

The creaks and the scratches
kept mom up all night in a worry.
Then up early for work,
tired and in a hurry.

We needed a guard,
and a dog would be best.
So we talked about what kind
and made boxes to check.

☐ OLD

☐ CALM

☐ PROTECT

☐ NICE

Our dog would be older, and calm, quite stoic-
but could hop up, bark and protect at a quick notice.

We took our list and headed to the pet store,
for a guard and companion that we would adore.

When we walked in the entrance,
the barks heard were insane!
We covered our ears and walked
down the lane.

We got to the dogs and what did we see? The loud one was jumping against the cage trying to break free.

Forget the list, this one's it,
I just know! He looks like he's
wearing a tux, and is only
missing the bow.

I look at mom and instantly start pleading.
She shakes the list we brought,
sternly reading.

"Just take him for a walk", the pet lady said.
I looked back and "no", mom was shaking her head
- "fiiiiiiine" she said.

We had him on a leash, an energetic young pup.
Mom was tired and pulling just trying to keep up.

I loved him already and we were racing down an aisle.
I looked back and could see mom softened at my laugh and smile.

Just then a man came around the
corner pretty sketch,
and the dog jumped between us
ready to protect.

My mom crumbled up the list and grabbed a few toys. She did the paperwork and now he's our boy!

FILL IN LIST FOR A NEW DOG

Our new dog MUST*:

☐ _____

☐ _____

☐ _____

☐ _____

☐ _____

*Compliance to this list is not necessary, and disregarding this list may result in a good time.

Please consider adopting from your local pet shelter!

Casper was found scavenging for food on Halloween. He was severely underweight. He is so friendly, they decided to name him "Casper" like the friendly ghost. We adopted Casper Nova on November 3, 2018.

Share your adoption stories with us to be featured on our website!

Scan the QR code or go to www.CrazyDaisyandDisasterCasper.com

About the Author

Kristen is a mother and wife above all. She spent a few chaotic years as a single mother, which drives her passion to encourage and support other mothers doing it all. Always aspiring to make lemonade out of lemons, she shares her stories with joy of hard (but good) times. She is currently a program manager who has many hobbies; sewing for her daughter (& Casper bows too), working out and doing anything outdoors. She is a Navy veteran and was stationed on the USS Theodore Roosevelt and was operating in the engine room when we landed the first drone on an aircraft carrier. She has found a missing person, been on world news, and even performed a wedding ceremony for one of her best friends. She is a strong believer in "Where there's a will, there's a way!", and knows no limits.

Printed in Great Britain
by Amazon

23780553R00016

HEY JU?

A Story About Music, Superheroes and Bugs

Chuck Neighbors
illustrated by Beth Niquette

Hey Jude

For Jude

"Mercy, peace and love be yours in abundance."
Jude 1:2 (NIV)

When I was born, my mom and dad gave me my name.

Hey Jude.

People seemed to like my name. In fact, they liked it so much they would sing my name instead of just say it.

I found out that Hey Jude is not only my name, but also a song that lots of people know.

It was kinda nice but kinda strange that people would sing my name.

They would sing, "don't be afraid."

This actually kinda scared me. I wasn't afraid until they sang, "don't be afraid." Now I wonder why they said that!

My older sister is named Lucy in the Sky with Diamonds. It's a long name, so I just call her Lulu. Lots of people sing her name too, but not as much as they sing Hey Jude.

I found out that *Lucy in the Sky with Diamonds* is also a song. Both *Hey Jude* and *Lucy in the Sky with Diamonds* are songs by some beetles.

I guess my mom and dad must like beetles.

I like bugs and I've seen beetles. My Nana gave me a special jar for collecting bugs. She helped me collect some beetles in the jar. I wonder if these were the beetles that sang *Hey Jude* and *Lucy in the Sky with Diamonds*.

It seems weird that beetles would sing songs that people would know about.

But I'm just a little boy…I have a lot to learn about bugs and songs and stuff.

I have two uncles that I like a lot. When I see them they call out, "Hey Jude - The Dude."

Sometimes they just say, "The Dude." I guess that is called a nickname. I like being "The Dude."

My Dad likes to collect toys. He has lots of superhero toys. My favorites are Spiderman and Hulk.

When I visit with Nana and Papa they like to play *The Spiderman Theme Song*. It's my favorite song. When they play the song I like to pretend that I am Spiderman.

I wonder if this song is by the beetles too?

I really like songs. Maybe when I grow up I can write songs like *Hey Jude,* and *Lucy in the Sky with Diamonds*...and *Spiderman.*

♪♪♪Spiderman♪♪♪

I want a super power just like Spiderman. Maybe I can be Beetleman. I could fly up in the sky, protect people with my hard shell...

My Papa said my name is ancient—that means very old—like Papa. He said the name means "praise." He says praise means to say nice things about someone and the things they do.

My Nana does nice things for me. *Hey Jude*, the song even talks about her. Maybe it is a song to praise my Nana.

It's nice to have a song about me and my Nana.

Hey Jude, that's me.

You can call me The Dude, or Beetleman if you want.

But I'm Hey Jude...or just Jude for short!

Children's Books by Chuck Neighbors

I Am Lucy

Where is Lucy?

The Rescue of Jonathan Dough

Printed in Great Britain
by Amazon